How to Conker the World

D1158609

How to Conker the World

KATHY ASHFORD

Illustrated by Paul Parks

TIGERS

Andersen Press • London

First published in 2004 by
Andersen Press Limited,
20 Vauxhall Bridge Road, London SW1V 2SA
www.andersenpress.co.uk

British Library Cataloguing in Publication Data
available
ISBN 1 84270 321 8

Phototypeset by Intype Libra Ltd
Printed and bound in Great Britain by
Bookmarque Ltd, Croydon, Surrey

Chapter 1

'HOW TO CONKER THE WORLD by Seb Markham.'

Yes, that was it!

Seb had never felt like this before. Not in his whole life. Actually wanting to do his homework. Of course the teacher hadn't meant to give the class anything exciting to do. Seb knew that. It was when the third conker swung off its string in the middle of the lesson and struck Miss Jones on the back of the neck that her nerves had finally snapped.

'What th . . . Right!' she shrieked, rubbing her neck. A deep red patch marked the spot where the conker had struck. 'You'll do three hours' homework every night this week. I want twenty tried and tested uses for horse chestnuts that do not involve whirling them around on bits of string. Dismissed!'

Ideas were simply flooding into
Seb's head as he rushed along the
street. He wouldn't just write a couple
of sides, he would write a whole book,
with real chapters. He'd prove just how
useful conkers were, for everything.
He'd show everybody how to conker
the world.

'Hey, Seb, where're you off to? Wait
for me.' A large boy with spiky blond
hair came lumbering up.

'Can't stop, Spike.'

'What? We were gonna try and get some more rubber bands out of that postman, remember? I still need loads to finish my rubber band ball.'

'Yes, but not now. Got all this homework, haven't we?'

'You're not gonna do it, are you?' said Spike, jaw dropping in disbelief.

'We . . . ell,' Seb faltered.

'Boffin!' said Spike.

He turned on his heel and stalked off down the street.

For a moment, Seb was tempted to go after his friend, but the sheer weight of the conkers in his bulging pockets reminded him that he had other things to do.

The rubber bands would have to wait. But where was he going to get enough conkers to do some really good experiments? After all it was quite late in the season now. Seb thought hard.

He knew of some brilliant trees, but getting at them could be a bit risky.

Chapter 2

A few minutes later and he was back home. Opening the front door, he called out in his most innocent voice.

'Helloo-oo! Mu-um? Da-ad? I'm ho-ome!'

Seb's sing-song tone was enough to arouse anyone's suspicions, but fortunately for him, there was no reply.

Seizing his chance,
Seb raided the
fridge, the biscuit tin
and the fruit bowl
before munching his
way to his bedroom.
Flopping down at the

mountain of rubbish which passed for
a desk, he peeled an old
piece of chewing gum
off the pock-marked
window, popped it into
his mouth and gazed out.
Not twenty metres away
stood two of the most beautiful horse
chestnut trees
you could
imagine.

Wonderful specimens,
weighed down with spectacular conkers.
There was only one problem. The trees
were in next door's garden. Seb and
Mr Smith were not exactly the best of
friends. Not since the incident with the
ball of fire. Then there'd been the
superjet hose. That had been rather
unfair, thought Seb. It wasn't his fault
that Mr Smith had come round the

corner just as the hose came on. And
Seb had stopped the water jet when
Mr Smith was only six feet off the
ground, so there was no real harm
done. But relations between them had
been strained ever since. No, they were
certainly not on conker-sharing terms.

Seb's neighbour was a problem and
a very present one at that. For, gazing
out of his window, Seb could clearly
see the gleam of Mr Smith's bald head

as he bent over a flowerbed a short distance from the conker trees. Mr Smith would have to be distracted. Just long enough for Seb to climb the fence, shin up the tree, bend the branches over towards his own garden and shake them so that the conkers fell onto 'home territory'. At this moment, Earless, Seb's dilapidated cat, avalanched onto the desk, cascading sweet wrappings, useful nails and old sandwiches everywhere.

'Stupid cat,' muttered Seb. 'Wait a minute though, you've given me an idea . . .'

Seb opened his window and leaned out. Smiling sweetly, he addressed his neighbour.

'Err, sorry to bother you.'

Mr Smith straightened up and glared ferociously up at him. Grasping his favourite conker firmly in his right hand, as if to draw courage from its cool, smooth shape, Seb continued.

'I just wondered if that cat was meant to be in your house? Saw it through the window squatting on your carpet. I think it might have been about to . . .' He let his voice trail off. If there was anything Mr Smith disliked more than Seb, it was cats.

The result was electric. Mr Smith reeled backwards,

gaped at Seb for a moment, then ran off towards the house, bellowing like a wounded rhino.

Seb had never actually heard a rhino bellow but he was pretty sure it would have sounded just like this. He was in business. He slipped through the fence, climbed up the tree and set to work.

Chapter 3

It was a tough job. Seb reckoned he
had about half an hour before anyone
else would come home and that he
would need four
wheelbarrow
loads of conkers.
Getting the
conkers
from the
garden up
to his room

proved to be harder than he'd
expected. But, Seb told himself, they
probably needed a new front door
anyway, and wasn't Dad always
complaining about the number of
ornaments in the hall? Whoever

designed wheelbarrows had obviously forgotten that they'd have to go up staircases. Seb took out a section of the banisters by his sister Milly's room to get the barrow through.

Some time later, he was surveying the pile of conkers on his bedroom floor. The smell was wonderful, like having your own tree in your bedroom. The reddish-brown sheen of the horse chestnuts reflected off the walls creating a gentle orange glow. For a moment Seb imagined himself as a pirate chief, sitting amidst an enormous pile of ancient gold. But no, these were conkers and he'd better do

something with them quickly.
'Trouble is,' said Seb to
himself, 'now I've got them up
here, where am I going to put
them all?' Just how do you store

fifty kilos of conkers in your bedroom so that there's a reasonable chance your mum won't hit the roof?

Seb's drawers, cupboards, pockets and socks were soon full. He had to take most of his clothes out of course. But he found a temporary home for them in dustbin bags outside the back door. He stuffed half the conkers into the hammock that swung from his ceiling, but it did mean that you could only move around the room on all fours. He was also a little concerned about the aquarium. Could fish survive sharing the tank with all those conkers? The speckly goldfish, Homer, was mouthing things at him

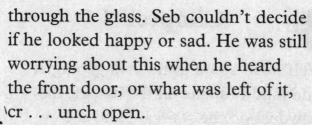

through the glass. Seb couldn't decide
if he looked happy or sad. He was still
worrying about this when he heard
the front door, or what was left of it,
cr . . . unch open.

'Seebbaaaastiaan!' Half the street
must have heard the shout. Seb crept
out of his room and peered round the
broken banister.

'Er, hello, Dad, you're
back early.'

Chapter 4

Seb's dad stood in the hall gaping at the muddy stains on the carpet, the sawdust on the staircase and the shattered ornaments. He was shaking all over, the remains of his hair stood on end, and, as Seb watched, the first three buttons on his dad's shirt shot off. Although his mouth was opening and shutting, no sound was coming out. That reminded Seb of something. Ah yes, that was it, Homer the goldfish.

But sadly, the silence was short-lived.
For Seb's dad was now joined by his
mum and things got loud, very loud
indeed.

'What the . . . ?' said his mum.

'. . . blazes are you up to?' finished
his dad.

'It's conkers,' said Seb.

'What have you done to our house?' said his dad.

'It's homework,' said Seb.

'How dare you?' said his mum.

'Miss Jones told us to . . .' said Seb.

'Enough!' said his dad. 'No television, no tea, no pocket money, no sweets, no friends round, no fireworks party, no birthday presents, no Christmas presents . . .'

'And that's just for starters,' finished his mum.

'Now, get up to your room,' said his dad.

'And get rid of any conkers . . . or . . . or . . . or else!' said his mum.

'Bloomin' horse chestnuts,' said his dad. 'We all know who's the nut around here.'

Chapter 5

It could have been worse, thought Seb, at least they hadn't looked in his room. Best to get on with the project as quickly as possible before they thought of coming up. Swiftly, and with the utmost concentration, he produced hundreds of tiny diagrams on his sister's giant sketch pad. One shape appeared again and again amid the signs and arrows that adorned each diagram, the smooth, rounded form of the common horse chestnut.

A loud bang on the front door
shattered the peace. The aggrieved
tones of Mr Smith drifted up the stairs
ominously. Then Seb heard his dad's
response. He sounded rather annoyed
too.

'Frankly, Mr Smith, if it's cats you
hate and there wasn't one there, I
don't really see what you're
complaining about.'

The front door slammed shut,
sending the broken letterbox rattling to
the floor. Seb's dad was coming

upstairs. Seb kept his head down and after a few moments, his dad walked slowly back down. Seb heard him talking to his mum in the garden.

'I went up there to sort Seb out once and for all. But there's something very odd about him. I mean odder than usual. He really does seem to be doing homework. Like he said. Should we call the doctor or something?'

'Well, maybe we should leave it a day or so. But if he's still at it by Thursday, I'll take him down to the surgery.'

Chapter 6

Seb was certainly 'at it' the next day. He'd planned all his conker chapters and it was time to start testing a few things out. It was shortly after breakfast that members of his family began to suffer the impact of his experiments. To be precise it was Gran who suffered it first. Walking down the garden path, she was hit plum on the forehead by a prize conker.

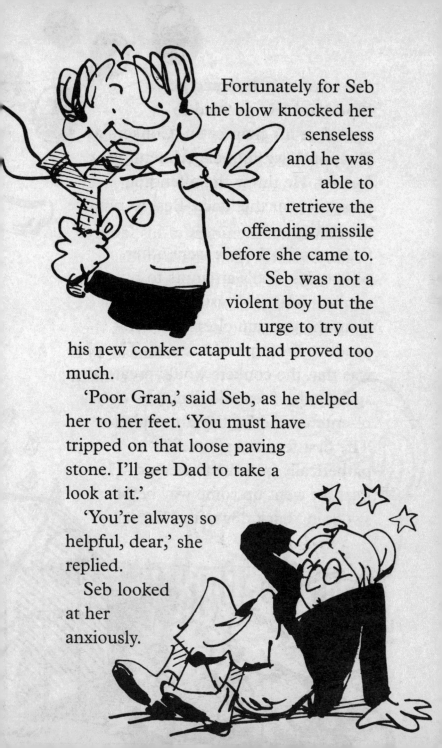

Fortunately for Seb the blow knocked her senseless and he was able to retrieve the offending missile before she came to. Seb was not a violent boy but the urge to try out his new conker catapult had proved too much.

'Poor Gran,' said Seb, as he helped her to her feet. 'You must have tripped on that loose paving stone. I'll get Dad to take a look at it.'

'You're always so helpful, dear,' she replied.

Seb looked at her anxiously.

She *must* have bumped her head hard. He decided to complete his chapter on 'Conkers as Weapons', without experimenting further. He threw the offending catapult over the fence. Best to remove the evidence.

After school there were other difficulties. Seb's attempts to put conkers into orbit using the motor from the vacuum cleaner did not produce the expected results. The plan was that the conkers would create a spectacular firework display as they re-entered the Earth's atmosphere. The first few had spurted pathetically into the flowerbed. The next lot went up some way before swooping back down and hitting

the greenhouse roof, with shattering
consequences. Seb carefully adjusted
the angle on the launcher. That was
better, hundreds of conkers
disappearing into the evening
sky. He waited,
expectations high.
But there was no
sign of them
reappearing.
   'Surely
what goes

up must come down? But when?' It was disappointing. This was to have been his most exciting experiment, and now he'd never know if it had worked or not. Seb hated leaving things up in the air like this. To add to his gloom, he suddenly noticed that the black binbags containing his belongings had gone from outside the back door. Swinging round, he caught a glimpse of the dustbin lorry disappearing round the corner in the road.

Well I needed some new stuff anyway, he thought to himself. Still, I won't tell Mum and Dad just yet.

Chapter 7

It was time to move on, and Seb set to
work on 'Conker Vehicles'. This
chapter started off rather well. The
conker raft floated beautifully and, if
she had only kept still, he was sure the
rabbit would have reached the other
side of the pond safely. The
skateboard, however, was not so
successful. He had to find lots of

conkers
of the
same size,
line them all up
carefully on a hill
and balance the tray
on top of them. Then he
had to jump on quickly
before the whole lot
careered down the
slope without
him. The first

time he tried it he
lost control and
ended up on the
pavement in the
arms of a
bemused, and
rather too
familiar,
passer-by.

'Sebastian!' said Miss Jones, rubbing
her bruised shin. 'I might have
guessed. And with some conkers. Well
you can just thank your lucky stars
you're not in school or I'd . . .'

'Sorry, Miss Jones, I'm just doing
my homework.'

'Homework! And I'm a Martian.
Just you wait!'

Seb didn't like the sound of this
at all. Worried that Miss Jones
might decide to pay a call
on his parents, he
watched until she had
hobbled out of sight.

Now it was more important than ever that his conker project was good. To avoid any further embarrassment, he decided to test the skateboard out at the back of the house. This time he ended up with a rather nasty bump on the head.

'Poor Seb,' said his mum, not looking at all concerned. 'Oh, but how interesting, that lump's exactly the same shape as a conker. You could write about it in your project!'

Seb gave his mother a withering stare. Parents!

Chapter 8

The next chapter was 'Conkers as
Medicines'. Seb found his family
strangely uncooperative on this
subject. His mother point-blank
refused to try the conker shell potion
he had cooked up to cure her stomach
ache. And oddly enough when he'd
tried a little of it himself, he'd
developed a stomach ache of his own.

It left a foul taste in his
mouth. Funny, because the
shell of a conker didn't really
taste of anything. Probably a bit
like polished wood. He licked the arm
of the kitchen chair so that he could
compare flavours. And at that precise
moment Milly walked in.

'Mum, come here quick, Seb's
eating the
furniture!'
She could be
a real pain
sometimes. In the
end, Seb decided
to stick to
writing about how
conkers could be

used to stop you getting ill in the first place, like dangling them from your hat to keep nasty flies off when you visited Australia. He'd been trying the prototype out when Spike walked by.

'Hey, Spike! What d'you think of my hat?'

'Wicked! With ideas like that, nothing can hold you back. You'll be putting them into orbit next.'

'No need to go all sarcastic. And actually I have . . .' But Spike had gone. He wasn't going to be brought round that easily.

The chapter on 'Conkers as Building Materials' stretched Seb's creative powers to the limit and he didn't have as much to show for his efforts as he would have liked. It was pretty obvious why nobody had thought of building things out of oval shapes before. He ended up with a structure that made the Leaning Tower of Pisa look dead straight. However, 'Conkers in Stories' was more successful. He managed to keep this experiment going all week and the results were startling. Miss Jones was bound to be impressed. By Friday he could say for sure that the

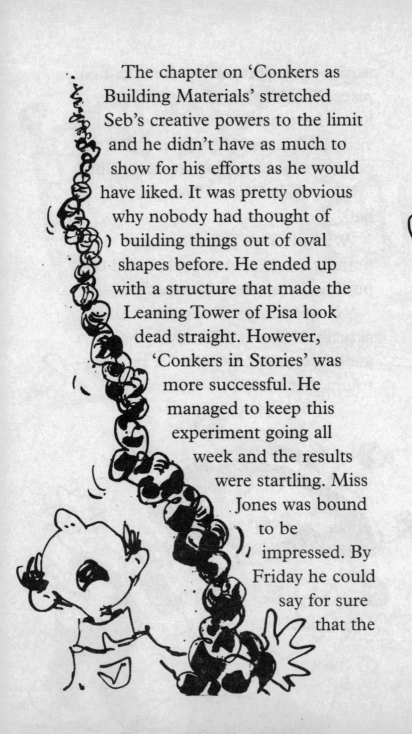

story of the Princess and the Pea was
true. He had placed a small conker
under his parents' mattress every night
of the week and neither of them had
noticed a thing. So you obviously had
to be a princess to feel a bumpy
mattress. It was a bit disappointing to
find there was no royal blood in the
family. Determined to do a thorough

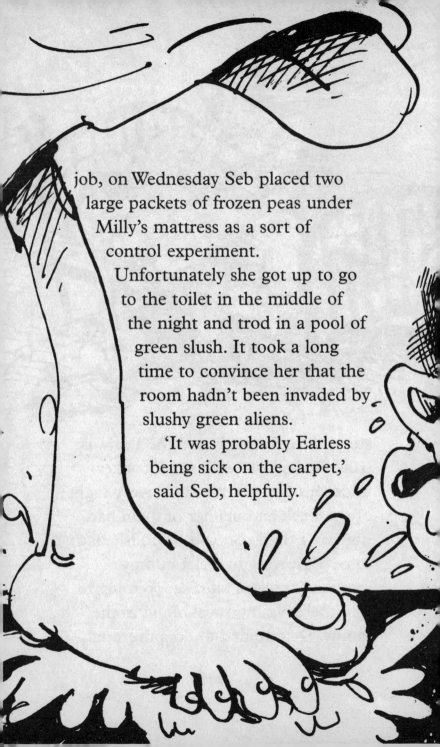

job, on Wednesday Seb placed two
large packets of frozen peas under
Milly's mattress as a sort of
control experiment.

Unfortunately she got up to go
to the toilet in the middle of
the night and trod in a pool of
green slush. It took a long
time to convince her that the
room hadn't been invaded by
slushy green aliens.

'It was probably Earless
being sick on the carpet,'
said Seb, helpfully.

Chapter 9

On Thursday night he sat in his room
putting the finishing touches to the
project. Despite all the problems, he
had pages of ideas and he'd really
enjoyed himself. It was a shame that
the family didn't feel the same. Really
they did make a lot of fuss about
nothing. Dad could have avoided the
broken leg if he'd just kept his eyes
peeled coming downstairs. Milly's

budgerigar had
eventually grown
rather fond of sitting
on those shiny, brown,
if rather unproductive,
eggs. And Seb had very
quickly apologised for
putting the conkers into
the toilet – didn't they
have any sense of
humour at all?

'Seb, come here! Now!' It
was his dad. More trouble.

'Here we go,' said Seb, as he made
his way downstairs, project in hand.

'There's a visitor. Friend of yours I
think,' said his dad, jabbing towards
the window with one crutch. Mr Smith
could be seen making his way
purposefully up to their front door.

'Oh dear,' said Seb, wearily.

'Whatever he wants, you sort it. And
if there's any trouble, any trouble at

all, you won't be seeing this again. Ever.' Before Seb could stop him, his dad seized the project and, turning clumsily on his one good heel, hobbled back into the lounge.

'You can't do that,' said Seb to his father's receding back. 'I've spent all week on it.'

Dejectedly Seb turned to face the front door. Mr Smith's face was now clearly visible through the glass panel.

But it looked different somehow.
Gosh, thought Seb, he seems to be
smiling. Seb cautiously opened the
door. Better get it over with.

'Was this yours?' said Mr Smith,
holding out Seb's conker catapult.
'Found it in my garden.'

'Err, maybe,' said Seb. 'I think so.'

'Well, young man, you surprise me. A generous thought. An ingenious design too. I persuaded the postman to give me a new rubber band and with that on it works even better. The cats certainly won't be bothering me again.'

Poor Earless, thought Seb. Still, if she'd got any sense, she'd keep out of his way.

'Oh, it's nothing. Glad you liked it.'
Seb smiled broadly. With Mr Smith
happy, Dad would have to return the
project.

'I'd offer you some conkers in
return,' Mr Smith continued, 'but
there don't seem to be any left on the
tree. Wretched squirrels!'

WILLIAM THE CONKEROR

CHAPTER X.

Chapter 10

Next day Seb set off happily for
school, project in hand. He felt
especially pleased with the front cover.
There was William the Conqueror, or
'Conkeror' as the caption read,
resplendent in shining armour,
whirling a conker straight into King
Harold's eye. Seb was confident that

53

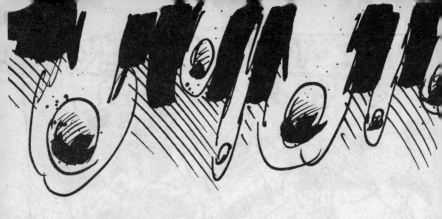

even Spike would be impressed by
what he'd done and they'd soon be
friends again.

It was a perfect day. The heavens
were a brilliant blue, and even now
rich, reddy brown conkers beckoned to
Seb from the avenue of horse
chestnuts in the park. But before he
could take a step in their direction a
strange thing happened. The sky

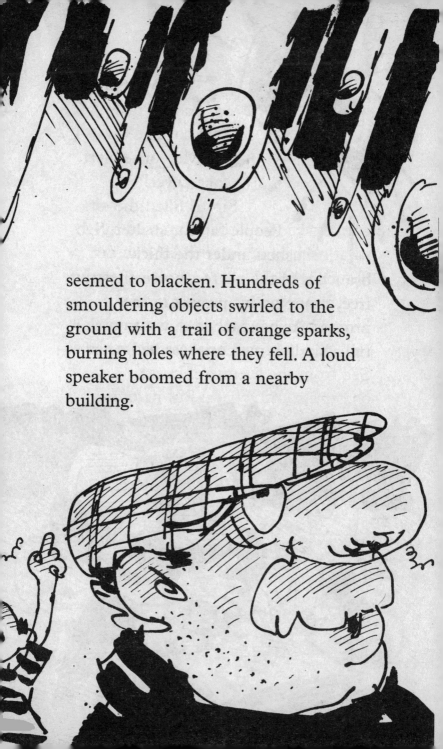

seemed to blacken. Hundreds of smouldering objects swirled to the ground with a trail of orange sparks, burning holes where they fell. A loud speaker boomed from a nearby building.

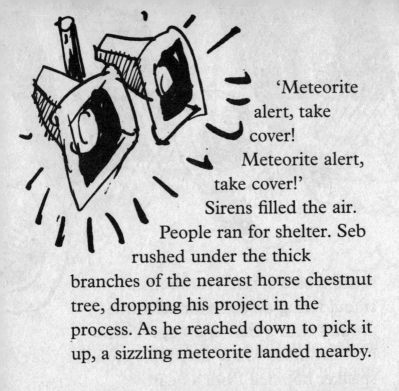

'Meteorite alert, take cover!
Meteorite alert, take cover!'
Sirens filled the air. People ran for shelter. Seb rushed under the thick branches of the nearest horse chestnut tree, dropping his project in the process. As he reached down to pick it up, a sizzling meteorite landed nearby.

Seb glanced quickly up into the tree,
loaded with shiny conkers, then down
again at the brown, burnt-out shell.
They were about the same size. His
jaw dropped, maybe it wasn't a
meteorite shower
after all.

  'Hey, Seb, you
idiot! Get moving, it's
meteorites!'
Spike rushed
past making
for the nearest
building.

'No way. If we shelter we won't see
my fireworks properly. Said I'd got
them into orbit, didn't I?'

Spike stopped and gazed at his
friend with renewed respect. 'You
didn't? Wicked! Wish I'd had a go
myself now. Still, you
won't be able to give
the project to
Old Jonesy
today. She's off
sick. Really bad
leg – some idiot

ran into her in the street.'

'It's like an invasion, worse than the Blitz,' said an old man, dodging the sizzling conkers as he hurried by.

'*How to Conker the World*. What goes up must come down!' said Seb, with quiet satisfaction.